MW00948585

Happy to Be Me

Positive Affirmations
for Little Boys

An ABC Book of Rhymes

By Sarah Mazor
Illustrated by K.S.Mallari

Thank you for purchasing

Happy to Be Me

I hope you enjoy the book
and read it often!

Copyright © 2019 MazorBooks

All rights reserved. No part of this book may be reproduced or
transmitted in any form or by any means, electronic or mechanical,
without the written permission from the author and the publisher,
except for the inclusion of brief quotations in a review.

AUTHOR'S NOTE

Happy to Be Me: Positive Affirmations for Little Boys offers 26 rhyming affirmations accompanied by lovely illustrations that will delight your child.

Positive affirmations are powerful and effective in building self-confidence, self-belief, and optimism in children. This well-documented impact of positive affirmations inspires parents to promote this habit in their children's daily routine.

Read *Happy to Be Me: Positive Affirmations for Little Boys* with your son, grandson, nephew or favorite godchild, and watch as your beloved little boy blossoms.

Also available:
Happy to Be Me: Positive Affirmations for Little Girls and *Happy to Be Me: Positive Affirmations for Little Kids* (the combined version).

With gratitude,
Sarah Mazor

"Be silly.
Be honest.
Be kind."

~ Ralph Waldo Emerson

"You are you.
Now, isn't that
pleasant?"

~ Dr. Seuss

Aa

Adorable

I make faces and I giggle
I jump high and I wiggle
I am happy you see
I am ADORABLE me

Bb

Brotherly

I love my brother who's so small
I hold his hand so he won't fall
I am happy you see
I am BROTHERLY me

Curious

I ask and I inquire
To learn is my desire
I am happy you see
I am CURIOUS me

Dd

Darling

I am loved and I love back
I so love my uncle Jack
I am happy you see
I am DARLING me

Ee

Excellent

I tidy my desk and I tidy my bed
I put things away like Mommy said
I am happy you see
I am EXCELLENT me

Ff

Fearless

I am strong and I am brave
Fun adventures I crave
I am happy you see
I am FEARLESS me

Generous

I share my lunch with little Trudi
I even share my chocolate goodie
I am happy you see
I am GENEROUS me

Hh

Healthy

I jump rope and I play
I exercise every day
I am happy you see
I am HEALTHY me

Imaginative

I tell stories and funny tales
Of mermaids dolphins and whales
I am happy you see
I am IMAGINATIVE me

Jj

Joyous

When I play with Lil the cat
On the playroom's little mat
I am happy you see
I am JOYOUS me

Kk

Kindhearted

I gave my toy to Lilly May
Who broke her foot the other day
I am happy you see
I am KINDHEARTED me

Ll

Lovable

Mommy hugs me oh so tight
Daddy calls me his delight
I am happy you see
I am LOVABLE me

Mm

Mysterious

I have an invisible friend
With whom I play pretend
I am happy you see
I am MYSTERIOUS me

Nn

Neighborly

I sometimes visit friends next door
And play with Eric who is four
I am happy you see
I am NEIGHBORLY me

Oo

Optimistic

I'm always in a cheery mood
I smile a lot 'cause life is good
I am happy you see
I am OPTIMISTIC me

Polite

I say thank you and I say please
And God bless you when you sneeze
I am happy you see
I am POLITE me

Quick

I like to run with Jake and Brock
And race with them around the block
I am happy you see
I am QUICK me

Rr

Remarkable

I write and draw and also sing
But painting is my favorite thing
I am happy you see
I am REMARKABLE me

Ss

Silly

I like acting a little zany
Even though I am quite brainy
I am happy you see
I am SILLY me

Tt

Truthful

What I have done today and why
I'll tell you all for I don't lie
I am happy you see
I am TRUTHFUL me

U u

Unique

My sister my brother and I make three
But I am the only one that's me
I am happy you see
I am UNIQUE me

Vv

Valuable

I am a blessing says my mother
Like my sister and my brother
I am happy you see
I am VALUABLE me

Ww

Wonderful

I am nice and sweet and kind
The best that you may find
I am happy you see
I am WONDERFUL me

(e)Xtraordinary

I asked the letter X to ask the letter E
To let it use an E word to tell about me
I am happy you see
I am (e)XTRAORDINARY me

Yy

Yummy

I ate some ice cream with sugar and spice
It spilled on me so I smelled nice
I am happy you see
I am YUMMY me

Zz

Zippy

I learned a new word from Guy
It begins with a Z and ends with a Y
I am happy you see
I am ZIPPY (full of energy) me

Be Happy
Because
You
are
You
!

The ABCs
are done,
but can you think
of more words
that describe a
happy you?

List of More
'Happy to Be Me'
Words

_____

_____

_____

_____

_____

Look for the Girls Edition of
Happy to Be Me

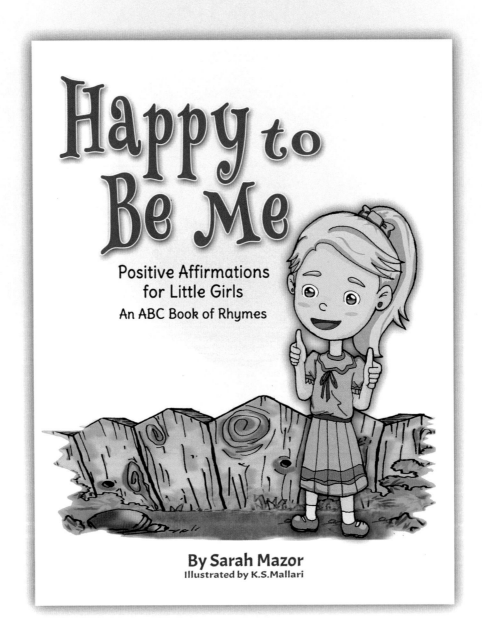

Available on Amazon

Visit the Growing
MazorBooks Library

Children's Books with Good Values

www.MazorBooks.com

www.mazorbooks.wordpress.com
www.facebook.com/mazorbooks
www.twitter.com/mazorbooks

51529747R00022

Made in the USA
Middletown, DE
03 July 2019